Camelia Lica

The Little Girl
and the Balloon

Illustrated by Anda Cofaru

May 2014

ISBN: 978-1499-2964-64

To my little girl, Stephanie, with love.

Come, Balloon,
Give me your string,
Let us fly and laugh and sing!

Go, Balloon,
Your string I hold,
Let us fly where dreams unfold!

The Little Girl and the Balloon

This is the story of a Little Girl who loved a Balloon, and of a Balloon who only ever loved her.

The Little Girl

In a Big City, in an even Bigger Country, there lived a Little Girl. During the day, the City was full of hurried people, hurried cars, hurried trains. It was full of noise and tumult: the sound of footsteps, traffic, voices, honking and ringing phones filled the streets with a thunderous hum of activity. At night, the noise quieted and the City slept under a soft, fluffy blanket of whispered lullabies, beneath the star-filled sky. But the stars were scarcely seen, for the forever shining lights of the Big City covered them.

The Little Girl was a happy child. Every day she walked to school, backpack on, playing hopscotch with the invisible lines on the pavement or jumping on one foot, if the sidewalk wasn't covered in puddles from a recent rainfall (just between you and me, she quite liked jumping into the puddles, but she was afraid of getting her socks wet and being scolded by her Parents). She often strolled aimlessly, daydreaming of all the dreams swirling through her curl-covered head. She had many dreams. They were hers and hers alone, dreams that she was afraid to share with others. One day at school, she shared one of them with a few classmates and they laughed at her. They said she was young and naïve, even though she was their age. She blushed fiery red, like a poppy, and laughed with them. She told them it was a joke. After all, who would believe such a thing? From that moment, she hid inside all these colorful thoughts and dreams, that were like the glow of a living rainbow, keeping her company. She enjoyed playing with them, especially in the evenings. Then, she liked looking through the window at the night sky, even though the stars were hard to see through the luminous fog of the City. The Little Girl knew, however, what the real starry sky looked like, because once during a holiday with her Parents she left the Big City and went up a tall mountain. She climbed all day. So big was that mountain that it seemed to reach the sky. When they finally reached the top, it was nighttime and they had to camp there. That was the first time the Little Girl had seen the real night sky. She had opened her eyes wide, astonished by how many of the little flickering lights were in the sky. She wondered who lit them up at twilight and put them out at dawn. She thought the Moon lit them up and the Sun switched them off. She didn't even ask her Parents, because there could be no other way.

But in the Big City, when night comes and she slips in her warm bed, the Little Girl starts to dream. These are not the dreams brought on by sleep, but ones dreamt with eyes wide open – colorful dreams that know neither rest nor sleep. And despite those dreams, sometimes, but only sometimes, she feels a little lonely.

The Balloon

One cheerful spring day, while returning from school, the Little Girl took the long way home through a lovely park full of colorful flowers. What a magnificent day it was, full of beauty and song. Flowers hummed, birds chirped, grass rustled, spring insects buzzed and a soft wind was winding through trees bursting in pink, white and green. The Little Girl skipped happily along lively paths, in tune with the music of the pastel-hued wind around her.

"Just look at this big-bellied bumblebee! Such a small bird, but how enchanting her chirp is! I wonder, did that yellow flower really wink at me then bashfully lower her head? Ah, how big and shiny are the leaves on the tree ahead!"

"One, two, three,
Birdies in a tree!
Four, five, six,
The wind is playing tricks!
Seven, eight, nine,
This game is mine!
And now comes ten
So I'll start again!"

"Yet, are they really leaves? I thought I just saw them blink! Ah, it was just the sunlight was shining in my eyes."

"One, two, three…"

"Good spring to you!" a little voice suddenly called from the tree with blinking leaves. The Little Girl was not at all startled, but simply looked up surprised. Behind the May flowers, perched in the branches, a big green Balloon was looking at her, equally amazed.

"Good spring to you as well," she answered politely, a little intimidated. "Who are you?"

"Me?" asked the Balloon, puzzled. "I'm a Balloon! Who are you?"

"I'm a Little Girl. Why are you so excited, Balloon? Haven't you seen children before?"

"Oh, yes, yes! Of course I've seen children before," answered the Balloon, coughing lightly

4

to mend his voice. "But I've never seen a Little Girl quite like you!" said he, distracted, swaying slightly in the wind.

The Little Girl smiled and blushed fiery red, like a poppy, as she always did when she was overwhelmed.

"What do you mean, like me?" she chirped happily, daring to look into the Balloon's big eyes.

"What do you mean, what do I mean? Hm. So pretty and full of spring."

"I thought you were a flower," he added slowly, sighing and closing his eyes.

It was then that the Little Girl noticed that the Balloon was not really green, but that his eyes were so green that, when they opened, their color spread like a light, all around. It was clear to her that she had never seen such a Balloon. And, evidently, she had never encountered one that could talk! But this held little surprise for her, as, in her world, the one she created in her curly-haired head, many such wonderful things could and did take place. Nevertheless, this was the strangest thing to ever happen to her!

A puzzled silence followed for a few moments, while the Balloon, swaying slightly in the wind with his eyes closed, sighed quietly and pretended to bathe lazily in the sunlight. He was waiting to see what the Little Girl would say, wanting to continue the conversation.

"Where are you from, Balloon?" the Little Girl asked, in order to fully understand the situation.

"Where am I from? Where am I from?" chanted the Balloon dreamily, becoming once again shiny and green as he had opened his big eyes at the Little Girl's question. He seemed in no hurry to answer her, so the Little Girl continued impatiently:

"Do you come from Balloon Country?"

"Yes! Yes, I do come from Balloon Country!" the Balloon repeated happily. The Little Girl's question had puzzled him. He had no memory of coming from somewhere. In fact, he didn't remember ever existing in any place but here, in this beautiful song-filled park, since the beginning of spring.

Before… what happened before? Why bother with such things! With so many flowers around and beside such a wonderful Little Girl, who cared where he came from?

"You're beautiful," said the Little Girl, touched, and she reached up to him. Without a word, the Balloon quickly descended from the tree and placed his string in her hand. The Little Girl held it tightly and smiled.

"Do you want to be my balloon?" she asked.

The Balloon jumped with delight and answered immediately, in his little helium voice.

"Yes, from now on I'm your balloon!"

He was silent for a minute, then continued slowly:

"You know, I've never been someone's balloon. I'm happy to be your balloon."

"Do you want to go for a walk?" asked the Little Girl before she started down the lane, without waiting for an answer, pulling the Balloon along with her.

Butterflies and Flowers

"And what do you do all day, Balloon? Do you get bored, alone in a park so big?'

"Oh, no," answered the Balloon shaking his big head. "I'm very busy."

"Very busy with what?" the Little Girl asked curiously, as was her nature.

"Well, let me see. All day, I contemplate! And I'm not at all alone. The flowers on earth and the birds in the sky keep me company."

"Hmm…" the Little Girl hummed, preoccupied. The Balloon's answer made her pause. She continued quietly:

"I sometimes feel alone even when I'm with other children."

They walked quietly for a while, followed by a cheerful gust of wind.

"Tell me, Balloon, what do you contemplate all day long?" she resumed, shaking her curls in the golden sunlight.

"Everything that surrounds me. Even the flowers, who sit and chat all day!"

"What do you mean? Flowers can speak?"

"Of course they can! Flowers speak all the time! They're so talkative that sometimes they deafen me with their arguments. I have to draw their attention when their quarrels become too loud and draw me from my thoughts," said the Balloon smiling.

The Little Girl was amused by the idea of quarreling flowers.

"Why do they fight?" she asked.

"Oh, they argue about everything and nothing. Which one is the most beautiful, the most colorful, the most elegant, the most delicate, or which one has the most pleasing scent. Which one is the most popular, that is, the most visited by bees and butterflies. You know how flowers are – much too conceited!"

"No, I don't know, but I'm finding out. I thought flowers were delicate, quiet beings with nothing to say."

"Oh, no. All beings have something to say. You only have to pay attention and catch their interest."

"I see. How intriguing. You know, I adore ladybugs – they're very cheerful!"

"I like them too, but you should know they're a little scatterbrained. They always lose their black spots in the grass."

The Little Girl grinned.

"What about butterflies, are you friends with them?"

"I like butterflies a lot, even if they are but colorful puffs of wind. Today, they're here, and the next they're gone. They come and go. You could say they are like a fleeting dream. But they truly are beautiful."

"Yes, they are! I chase after them but I never try to catch them. I know they would be sad in my hand. They're very fragile, their wings break so easily. It's better to leave them in the air."

Having said this, the Little Girl started humming quietly and jumping joyfully on one foot. Suddenly, she had a thought.

"Surely, you don't like caterpillars?"

"Caterpillars? How could I not like them? The caterpillar is the journey towards the butterfly."

The Little Girl stopped humming, closed her eyes and repeated:

"The caterpillar is the journey towards the butterfly…"

"You know, Balloon, I never thought that way about caterpillars. They seemed so repulsive to me, looking like thick, green earthworms."

Then after moment of thought:

"Birds like caterpillars. I once saw a bird peck one from a branch and fly away. Now I'm sorry, you know, for the butterfly it could've become."

"I get along very well with birds!" boasted the Balloon. "They fly and chirp around me like I'm one of them! They're also very careful not to touch me with their sharp beaks. Sometimes they pick up my string and take me for a stroll through the sky. It's so enjoyable!"

"I would like to fly as well,' the Little Girl muttered dreamily. "Not on a plane, it's not the same. I would like to fly with you. To say 'go, Balloon', and for you to take me up! Do you think it's possible?"

The Balloon lowered his eyes sadly.

"I don't know. I don't think I'm strong enough. Any gust of wind can take me away. I have to tie my string to branches not to be swept away."

They both fell silent, each preoccupied with their own thoughts before the Little Girl cheered up suddenly.

"Do you want to play hopscotch?"

"What is hopscotch? I want to play with you, but you have to teach me."

"Look: you draw a few big squares on the pavement and then you jump from one to another, careful not to touch the lines with your shoes. I don't have any chalk with me but we can pretend that the whole path is a big game of hopscotch and jump from square to square! I always do this. What do you say? I will hold your string tightly, Balloon, so don't be afraid!"

The Balloon's eyes sparkled and he grew bigger and greener with delight.

"Then, let's play hopscotch!"

Take Me Home With You!

In a moment of forgetfulness, in the excitement of the game, a strong breeze snatched the Balloon from the Little Girl's hand and started drifting away with him.

"Oh, no!" said the Little Girl, scared. She worriedly called him back: "Balloon, come back! Balloon! Return to me!"

She chased after her new friend, who was blowing away in the wind. The Balloon had become transparent, for he had closed his eyes in fright.

The Little Girl had never been a good runner. She was the slowest in gym class, but now she fired up her legs and ran like crazy, her eyes fixed on her Balloon, which was still slowly moving away. She didn't even feel her knees getting scratched by branchy bushes, or the pebble in her shoe hurting her foot. She kept running until she got close to her Balloon, then she jumped up and caught his string.

"Phew," she panted, her heart still beating at a gallop.

"Phew," said the Balloon, who opened his eyes and became green once again. He had shrunk from fear and the Little Girl watched him worriedly.

Puff! Puff! She got to work and inflated her Balloon. He grew bigger and bigger, and greener, from happiness. What a wonderful friend he had found!

"I had never imagined the park was this beautiful," he thought happily. He swayed slightly, from right to left and from left to right, on the end of his string, to show the Little Girl the song echoing in his soul. And so they started walking again.

"What are you thinking of, Balloon?" the Little Girl asked.

"I'm not thinking of anything. I'm happy."

The Little Girl smiled. "What do you do when night comes, Balloon? Do you sleep?"

"Balloons don't sleep. At the very most, they take naps."

"But then, what do you do all night long, when flowers hide their faces in the petals and birds bury their heads in their feathers?"

"I watch the sky. Have you ever really looked at the sky? Have you seen how deep and full of stars it is? I can never get enough of watching it. And the Moon, so mysterious and distant, like an unwritten story. I truly do love the night sky," he finished dreamily.

"I do as well, Balloon! I can only see a small patch of it from my window, but I once climbed a tall mountain and I saw it from up high."

"One, two, three… Ah, Balloon, what was I thinking? It's late. I have to go home or my parents will be terribly worried!"

She became quiet, troubled, not knowing what to do. A shadow of sadness flashed through the Balloon's eyes, darkening his color. He hushed for a while, fidgeting anxiously on the end of his string.

"Could I come with you?" he asked quietly, becoming transparent once more. He had closed his eyes, as he always did when overwhelmed by emotion.

"To my house?" wondered the Little Girl, who had not thought of such a simple solution.

She came around immediately and burst into a blaze of happiness.

"But of course, Balloon! Certainly! I believed you wanted to stay here, in your park. I would be extremely happy to take you home with me, if that would make you happy as well!"

"From now on, my home is wherever you are,' whispered the Balloon, blushing suddenly. (Can you imagine how a blushing green balloon would look?)

"I live not far from here," the Little Girl explained while skipping happily and pulling the Balloon along with her.

"Look, do you see that two-story house? That's where I live. The upstairs window facing the street is the one from my room. I have a lot of toys in there. I don't really like dolls, but I have many, many stuffed animals. There are a lot of them in all shapes and sizes. I have two giraffes, a big one and a little one, three wolves – I love wolves and I'm not afraid of them, like everyone else – three cats, one white and another other black and the third is grey, two unicorns, and a talking parrot. His name is Pepe and he's very cute. The only problem is that he repeats the same thing over and over."

She shrugged.

"It's to be expected, he's also a toy. With you however, I will be able to talk!"

She smiled beautifully, but quickly continued.

"I didn't mean to say that you are my talking toy! No, no, Balloon! You're my friend! My only reliable friend."

"Yes, I'm your friend," the Balloon repeated light-heartedly. The idea of being upset at the Little Girl's words had never occurred to him.

I Watched Over Your Sleep

"We are here," said the Little Girl, stopping on the doorstep. She started wondering how she would enter the house with a talking Balloon. What would her Parents say? The Balloon sensed her hesitation and smiled understandingly.

"Is that your window? The one with the blue curtains? I will go through there, since I can fly. We balloons don't enter through the front door like humans." He proudly lit up bright green.

"Oh, of course!" she cheered, relieved. "I will run up and open the window. Wait here for a little bit." She then burst through the door. Once inside her room, she opened the window impatiently and made a shushing gesture with her finger. "Hush, Balloon, someone might hear us."

"Hushhh," hissed the Balloon seriously as he slipped into the room.

As the Little Girl had said, there were toys everywhere: on the bed, on the floor, in the cabinet in the corner. On the desk by the window, however, her school books and notebooks were waiting patiently in neat stacks, like the Teacher had taught her.

"Have a seat, Balloon," she said, and then laughed at how hilarious the invitation sounded. "I have a little homework to do for tomorrow. You can play with my toys so you don't get bored." The Balloon placed himself quietly near the desk.

"I don't want to play. I would like to watch you, if you don't mind. I've never seen so many books."

A moment later, the door opened and the Little Girl's Mother entered the room.

"Here you are!" she said, lovingly stroking her hair. "Who were you talking to?" She murmured inaudibly, trying to quickly come up with a believable explanation. But it was unnecessary. Her Mother saw the open notebook and continued, pleased:

"Ready for your lessons? Excellent, I'll call you down for dinner in half an hour," she said before quietly leaving the room.

The Little Girl was left open-mouthed. Mother had said nothing about her Balloon. It was like he didn't exist! Maybe she hadn't seen him – but he was right next to her! While he may have closed his eyes the moment he heard the door open, and had become transparent like the air, the Little Girl could see him even then.

"Interesting," she thought. "When his eyes are closed, it seems, my Balloon is an invisible Balloon. This could be useful in some situations. At the very least, it's better than having to explain to everyone that my Balloon can speak. I wonder if he knows only I can see him like that? I'm not sure I should mention it. He might feel offended. I've seen how sensitive he can be. Any breeze can blow him away! I have to pay attention and to take care of him. He's both my Balloon and my friend."

That night after dinner, the Little Girl fell asleep with these thoughts running through her curly-haired head. Beside her bed, swaying happily, was the biggest and most beautiful green balloon in the world.

At School

"Good morning, Balloon!" the Little Girl said cheerfully, jumping out of bed.

"Good morning! Good morning!" the Balloon said, smiling roundly. He had waited eagerly for the Little Girl to wake up. As you recall, Balloons never sleep – at the very most, they take naps.

The Little Girl washed her face with cold water, brushed her hair, put on her little dress, opened the window wide and told the Balloon: "Wait in front of the house, please. I will be there right away!" and she sprinted down the stairs.

During the walk to school, the Little Girl proudly held the Balloon by the string. He was admired by all the boys and girls passing her by on the way to their own schools. She told the Balloon to stay still and silent so he wouldn't draw much attention. That way, they could look like a perfectly normal little girl walking to school and holding an absolutely normal balloon by the string. Nothing odd there. So, being obedient by nature, the Balloon did what the Little Girl asked of him.

"Such a big Balloon you have there," one of her Classmates said, watching the Balloon enviously. "What do you plan to do with it? You know very well that you can't bring it to class with you."

14

"That's no problem," the Little Girl replied serenely. "He'll wait for me outside until class is over."

"Ha, ha, ha!" her Classmates laughed. "If the wind doesn't blow it away!" They kept laughing haughtily as they entered the school building.

The Little Girl grew worried. She looked at her Balloon, then around her to make sure they would not be overheard, pulled the Balloon down by the string, and whispered in a serious tone:

"Balloon, could you wait for me in the schoolyard until I finish class? I promise I will play with you then."

"Yes, yes!" the Balloon, who had a cheerful disposition, happily agreed.

"Tie your string to a branch and be careful not to be blown away," she continued. Afterward she fell silent, wondering whether or not she should share her thoughts.

"I will tell you a secret. It will be ours alone. If someone startles you, if you're scared and want to become invisible for a few moments, close your eyes and think of me," she whispered. "I think that only I can see you when you close your eyes. For everyone else you become invisible."

The Balloon's eyes grew wide in astonishment. Such a thing had probably never crossed his mind. He remained dumbfounded for a few moments, then, twitching gently on the end of his string, answered her wearing the biggest of smiles:

"Ohoho! But this is wonderful news! To vanish completely, in front of everyone, whenever you want! How quaint, I like it! Are you sure about this, my Little Girl?"

"Yes, yes, Balloon! I'm quite certain. I saw it last night when Mother was in my room. She didn't even notice you. If you knew how much I would like to become invisible sometimes! For instance, last week the Teacher asked me to solve a math problem on the blackboard and I could not solve it. I was in front of the whole class and I saw the other kids smiling with superiority. I was so embarrassed. I closed my eyes, thinking of how convenient it would be if I had the ability to vanish from sight so I wouldn't have to see the amused glances they were throwing at me."

"What happened after that?" asked the Balloon, who had darkened from anxiety.

"Nothing happened. Since that day, I've studied much harder so I'd never have to wish to disappear. That's all."

15

Go, Balloon!

"Let's run, Balloon!" called the Little Girl cheerfully, dashing out of the school. The Balloon descended quickly from the tree he had patiently waited for her in and let his string fall into the Little Girl's hand.

"I waited for you," he said. "I floated around the windows and peeked into your classroom from time to time to see you."

"Who are you talking to?" a passing Girl asked.

"Nobody. I'm talking to myself," said the Little Girl, smiling and proudly dragging the Balloon along.

"Such a big balloon!" exclaimed the Girl. "I'd like to have a balloon like yours, too," she said before leaving.

Reaching the park, the Little Girl started running around, delighted by the lively sunshine that embraced the nature around her.

"Go, Balloon!" she called out. Suddenly, she felt lifted up in the air with a jerk. She looked down and realized with amazement that her feet were hanging in the air. She was flying! She exclaimed in surprise and, shortly, the Balloon descended and put her back on the ground. The Little Girl's heart was pounding very, very fast and she couldn't find her words. She stuttered:

"W-what was that, Balloon?"

"I have no idea," the Balloon answered, as stunned as she was. "I started running at your words and up we were. I think I've become stronger. I hope I didn't scare you terribly."

"Scare me? No, no, that was amazing! I've never been able to fly like that, like a bird. You gave me wings, my Balloon. Thank you."

They both grew quiet, sorting out their thoughts.

"Let's try it again!" the Little Girl said enthusiastically, stamping her foot playfully. "Fly with me, Balloon!"

She felt a small jerk through the string, but nothing happened. "Fly, Balloon!" she shouted impatiently, a little disappointed. Again, the string twitched a little but the Balloon didn't budge.

"Go, Balloon," she said again and suddenly felt herself being pulled up, floating in the air.

16

How magical! Beneath, the colors of the earth were blending in a swirling carousel, getting further and further away. The Little Girl felt light like a feather floating in a gentle breeze. She felt no fear, not a drop of concern, only a big wave of happiness flooding her soul. Was she dreaming? Was she really flying above everything? Did her Balloon truly exist? When was she going to wake up from this extraordinarily beautiful dream?

"Come, Balloon,
Give me your string,
Let us fly and laugh and sing!
Go, Balloon,
Your string I hold,
Let us fly where dreams unfold!"

The Little Girl felt the white velvet of a cloud caressing her cheeks and shouted:

"Fluffy clouds we're passing by!
Oh, it's such a dream to fly!"

And so, they flew until they reached a rainbow and turned back. When time was up, the Little Girl quietly said to her friend:

"Our flight came to an end
Let's return, my truthful friend!"

And the Balloon obediently brought her back to the ground.

The Toy World

"Did you know that toys can talk?" asked the Balloon one bright and beautiful morning, smiling affectionately at the messy little head that had popped out from under the sheets.

The Little Girl's eyes widened. "What do you mean, they talk? To whom? Among themselves?'

"Yes, among themselves. As soon as you fall asleep, the toys come to life. They have a world of their own. I have witnessed it, night after night, while you sleep."

"Is that so?' the Little Girl asked. "While I sleep? What if I pretend to sleep and then take a peek at them from the corner of my eye? Could I see them?"

"No," said the Balloon decisively. "They don't bother to hide from me, but you would not be able to see them no matter how hard you try. The very moment you wake up, they become still again in the exact spot you left them before going to sleep. It's a rule of their world, from what I understand, that no child can see them. They live only at night – and their lives are fascinating!"

"What do you know…And what do they do?"

"You would think they play, but in truth toys are very serious. They talk and develop friendships, they read the books from your bookcase and go to school."

"They go to school? Where? Who is their teacher?"

"The giraffe, Giselle, and she's quite a stern instructor. She teaches all the other toys to read so they can read the books from your bookcase. The puppy Lusu and the kitten Paloma are the most studious. They've already read all your books and are waiting for you to buy new ones so they can read those as well. They were talking, last night, about how they would like to read other kinds of books, too. Books for older children, about countries far away that they've never heard of before. Books about unknown mountains and rivers and forests, about people from all corners of the world. Books about other time periods. But they have one golden rule: toys cannot read a book before the child who owns it has read it. And so, my Little Girl, all the toys are counting on you! The more books you read, the more books they can read too."

"The toys are counting on me,' she said musingly. "This is very interesting. It would've never crossed my mind. In fact, it's quite logical. I'm their owner. Tell me, what else do they do at school?"

"They tell each other what they did during the day. How you played with them, what games you invented together. It's the biggest honor for a toy to be chosen to play with you."

"Tell me, Balloon, do my toys say good things about me?"

"Oh, yes! They all have such good things to say about you! They're very happy to have a friend like you. There is only one thing they don't like, and all have complained about it."

"What is it, Balloon? Tell me, I need to know!"

"They get a little upset when you scatter them all over your room and leave them in a big mess. That, they don't like. They want to be neatly placed back in their proper spots after the game is over. It's part of their dignity as toys."

At this, the Little Girl looked down, ashamed.

"They're right, Balloon! It's not their fault. I should be taking better care of them. I'm their owner after all and they depend on me!" she said, shaking her curly-haired head. "Balloon, will you excuse me for a minute? I will be a little busy. I have to tidy up my toys! I want them to feel happy and like me even more. I'm their friend as much as they're mine!"

The String That Ties Us Together

"Did something happen?" the Balloon asked one day after seeing the Little Girl gloomily leaving the school gates.

The Little Girl didn't answer him, she simply took him by the string he gently deposited it in her hand. They walked in silence for a while, the Little Girl with her head bowed, counting the pebbles they passed by on the road. Her steps were no longer sprightly and full of joy and her eyes, usually two windows of sunshine, were now shadowed by a grey curtain of gloom.

"Oh, Balloon," she sighed suddenly, feeling small and dejected.

"What happened, my Little Girl? Tell me, please! I'm your Balloon, am I not? Whatever happens, your Balloon is always here, above you, sending sunshine and happiness down through his string to his Little Girl. I will never let you become sad."

The Little Girl traced an invisible circle on the ground with her right foot as she spoke.

"Today, at school, the whole class laughed at me,' she whispered tearfully.

The Balloon wisely kept silent, waiting for the Little Girl to continue. He could see how hard it was for her to collect her thoughts.

"They laughed because I'm friends with a balloon. Such a thing is unheard of! A balloon is nothing but a colorful casing filled with air. What can it do? It can just wobble in the air. Any breeze can blow it far away. How can you claim that something like this is your friend?"
Big round tears were flowing down her poppy red cheeks.

"I told them my balloon was different, not like the other ones at all! They all laughed harder and told me that all balloons are the same. They just have different colors. Mine just happens to be green."

She grew silent, her head lowered.

"Aha, so that's what happened," the Balloon muttered in his little voice, and started shrinking sadly. The Little girl doubted him. She wasn't happy with him. Did she not believe in their friendship anymore?

"My Little Girl, why be upset over words spoken by those who envy our happiness? They don't understand that we balloons are much more than our colorful wrappings."

He sighed deeply, his breath leaving him with a whistle. "I offered my string to you. I'm always here, at the other end, even if it can seem much too long sometimes. It is what binds me to you. Through it, we communicate our happiness and joy to each other. It's the link between our souls. Never forget that, my little friend."

His voice faded out, as his body was now deflating rapidly.

"Oh, no!" the Little Girl cried out anxiously. "Forgive me, Balloon, I'm sorry!"

Puff, puff, she started to breathe air and love into her dear Balloon.

"You're right, Balloon, I was being foolish! Why should we care about the others? They don't know you can speak, they don't know how we laugh together. Nor do they know how strong you are, that you can take me flying to the sky."

Puff. Puff.

"Only you make my heart sing, Balloon! Only with you I can fly to the stars and back. My Balloon, with eyes the color of spring grass! Don't deflate, please! Come back to me."

Puff. Puff. She breathed out with all her strength until the Balloon smiled once again, big and lively.

"Forgive me, Balloon," the Little Girl repeated. "How could I ever doubt you? You're my best friend and I want no other!"

"Only you, my green Balloon,
Took me flying to the Moon!"

"You know, I wonder," the Balloon said in a hushed tone. "Why do you think you're the only one that can see me when I'm overwhelmed and, as is my habit, shut my eyes? You told me that it's their light that makes me visible to the other ones. Why? Is it because only you know me well enough, only you understand my moods and emotions. I belong to you. You're my friend. You're my one and only Little Girl."

The Little Girl smiled widely, her eyes sparkling like twin stars. She pulled the Balloon downward by his string and hugged him with all her heart. She stuck her Little Girl cheek to his Balloon cheek, looked into his eyes and patted his big head. The Balloon grew bigger and bigger with happiness, swaying happily right to left and left to right on the end of his string. He was once again a beautiful and intense green.

"You're a wonderful Balloon," said the Little Girl, taking him by the string and slowly starting to walk on the path home.

Behind them, the park filled with the lively chirping of birds.

The Balloon With a Bowtie and Top Hat

"Close your eyes, I have a surprise for you!" the Balloon said cheerfully, tugging gently on his string. "You can open your eyes now," he called, eager to see her reaction.

The Little Girl gave a surprised and admiring "aah" and started clapping enthusiastically. The Balloon was all dressed up. He had a dashing black top hat on top of his head and wore a bright red bowtie around his neck.

"You look so handsome, Balloon!" exclaimed the Little Girl, skipping happily. "Your bowtie looks like a red butterfly in flight! And the top hat gives you a very distinguished air!"

"Oh my, oh my, oh my!
My Balloon wears a bowtie
And a beautiful top hat!
Who has seen balloons like that?"

"What is the occasion for this? Are we going to a party? Are we celebrating something?"

"Of course we are celebrating! It's our anniversary!"

"Our anniversary? How so?"

"I've just decided on it! Why not? Every day can be our anniversary! Every moment we spend together is to be celebrated. Now, allow me to offer you my string and invite you to fly to the Rainbow Falls," he said gallantly, in the proper manner for a Balloon wearing a bowtie and top hat.

"I shall gladly accept that invitation, Gentleballoon! If you could give me just a moment to smooth my dress, adjust my socks and polish my shoes.

"That's it. I'm ready to go."

"What are we waiting for?
Come my friend, let's fly away,
Let us both go our way!
Far away, Gentleballoon,
To the Stars and to the Moon!"

"I'm ready too. Grab my string and hold on, Little Earth Girl! Of course, you know what you have to do so we can take off. Speak the magic words and we will be there right away!"

"Come, Balloon,
Give me your string,
Let us fly and laugh and sing!
Go, Balloon,
Your string I hold,
Let us fly where dreams unfold!"

"Go!" sounded a little voice and the Little Girl felt herself float up, surrounded by a gentle breeze. "Go!" the voice sounded again, and at the other end of the vibrating string she was holding, the Little Girl saw her Balloon smiling down at her before he looked up to search the distance for the Rainbow Falls.
"What is beyond the Rainbow Falls, Balloon?"
"I don't know. Do you want to find out?"
"No, Balloon. I'm happy with the way things are!"

Balloons Go *POP!*

"Hey, look! It's the Little Girl with the balloon!"

"Hey you, how is your air-filled friend doing?"

A few of her Classmates laughed maliciously at her.

The Little Girl said nothing and passed them by, her gaze firmly locked ahead, pulling the Balloon along.

"Hey, I'm talking to you!" one of her nastier Classmates shouted, stomping her foot. "A flimsy balloon couldn't be much of a friend. Tell me, what will you do if one day it flies into a spiky bush and pops? Or if someone pokes it with a needle?"

"Ha, ha, ha!" the Others giggled, wriggling as if miming the action. "*POP, POP, POP!*"

The Little Girl stopped walking abruptly, furious. She turned around to face them, her cheeks flushed poppy red and shouted with all her might.

"My Balloon is big and strong and he will not break! He's smart, and takes care of me, and takes me flying to places you will never even know exist!"

That said, she spun around on her heels and ran away with her Balloon.

"Ha, ha, ha!" the harsh laughter from the Others followed her.

The Starry Sky

"Balloon, tonight, after everyone falls asleep, I want us to fly to the stars!"

"Of course, my Little Girl. The sky is my specialty!" boasted joyously the Balloon. "Allow me to get my hat and fix my bowtie. You cannot go to a party in the stars unprepared."

He smiled glowing a brighter green than ever.

The Little Girl smoothed her dress, adjusted her socks and polished her shoes. She opened the window wide and let out a delighted "aah" at the sight of the all stars brightening the night sky.

"Let us be on our way, then!
Go, Balloon,
Take me so high,
That my hand can touch the sky!"

"Gladly, my dear friend!
Little Girl, hold tight my string,
Let us fly, where stars can sing!"

"Fly away, fear not, Balloon,
Fly until we reach the Moon!"

Give Me a Star

"It's beautiful out here," the Little Girl said when they reached the Tall Mountain. Up there, nothing was blocking their view of the sky.

They stood, holding hands – or, string, for the Balloon, given what he is – gazing at the brightly-lit night sky.

"Balloon, give me a star so it would be only mine and yours when…" the Little Girl whispered, then stopped abruptly, troubled.

"When what?" the Balloon asked.

The Little Girl wouldn't answer.

"When I'm no longer here?" he continued quietly.

The Little Girl kept her silence.

"Why are you thinking of that?" he asked in a hushed voice.

The Little Girl shrugged.

"I don't know how long balloons live. Normal balloons have short lives. They break easily or they deflate. Last year, for my birthday, I received a lot of colorful balloons. They were pretty for a few days, then, the ones that had not already been popped became smaller and smaller and sadder and sadder. It was as if their lives were leaving them along with their air."

"I'm not one of those balloons. I will continue to exist as long as you believe in me. I know now why I appeared on that branch in the spring-filled park. Before you, there was nothing. I was made for you. I gave you my string and I will always be with you, since my life comes from your friendship and your love for me. Please, don't be sad. Now, give your Balloon your hand, put my string in your pocket and let us take a stroll under the stars. We are going to their party, are we not?"

"Balloon, do you promise that you will never leave me? That you will always be my friend?"

He sighed deeply.

"My dear Little Girl, I don't know how long I will live on this Earth of ours. I could be here for a few more moments, days or years. Nevertheless, if one day I were to disappear, I want you

33

to know that I will always be with you, even if you will only see me in memories or dreams. You will be able to feel my presence and know that I'm with you. And every time you miss me, you can press your hand to your window and look outside. While others will see nothing, you will behold a big green Balloon floating beyond the glass and whispering to you 'My Little Earth Girl'."

"And now," said the Balloon formally, after a pause. "I will give you not a star but a planet! And not any planet, but the biggest one in the solar system! Ta-da! Do you see that dot, the brightest one in the sky? It's Jupiter. It will be our planet from now on."

"It's so beautiful! Is it really the biggest one? Why a planet and not a star? What are the stars, Balloon?"

"Stars are far away suns. They're so far from us that their light needs a long time to travel here. So much, in fact, that by the time that light arrives, they could be long gone. That's why I'm giving you a planet. A big, beautiful one. One that you can easily see in the sky. Most nights, it can be gazed upon, always proud and radiant. It could be no other way. After all, it's named after the biggest and most powerful god: Jupiter. Oh, when Jupiter got angry, big thunderstorms were unleashed on the world!"

"You know so many things, Balloon. Thank you for teaching them to me. Our friendship truly does seem like a fairy tale."

The Balloon swayed proudly on the end of his string. "And now, the time comes for us to have fun, my Little Girl. Do you want to swing from the Moon? It's the first day of the Crescent Moon, so it's a perfect time for it. I could tie my string to one end and make you a swing."

"Is that really possible, my Balloon? I never knew something like that could be done," the Little Girl said enthusiastically, clapping happily.

The Balloon smiled. "In our world, anything is possible. You only have to let your imagination fly."

The Others

"My dear Balloon," the Little Girl said affectionately, pulling the Balloon down by his string in order to caress his big head. The Balloon glowed like a gem and swayed happily from right to left and left to right on the end of his string.

The Little Girl kept silent, preoccupied by the thoughts swirling through her curl-covered head.

The Balloon stopped swaying, seeing that this was going to be a serious discussion.

"What is bothering you, my Little Girl? Tell your Balloon."

"My Balloon, I want to ask you something," she started solemnly.

"You can ask me anything, my little friend!"

"My Classmates, they laughed at me again. They said that I talk to myself and that I'm pretending to speak to a balloon. The whole School knows, and now even the Younger Children laugh when they see me in the hallways. They elbow each other and point at me. Oh, Balloon, I want to prove them wrong! I want them to get to know you. I want you to talk to them and to see the amazement in their eyes when you say: 'My name is Balloon. Pleased to make your acquaintance.' I would like to see them try to mock me after that! Will you do this for me, Balloon? Please."

The Balloon was quiet for a long time, and all the while his body kept deflating and his color became paler and paler.

"My Little Girl,' he started gently, in his little helium voice. "I thought you were happy with us, exactly as we are. Whatever the Others think is no concern of ours. Why are you not content keeping me to yourself? Why do you want to show me to the Others? Is that not vanity talking instead of friendship?"

He fell silent and let out a long sigh, then resumed.

"Of course, if you want to introduce me to Everyone, I will do as you wish. After all, you're my Little Girl."

"Thank you, Balloon," she said simply, and pulled him down by the string to happily kiss his forehead.

I Introduce to You, My Balloon!

"This is my friend," the Little Girl declared proudly to the crowd of Other Children surrounding her in the schoolyard. "He's not an ordinary balloon, but an enchanted one," she continued. "In fact, I will let him introduce himself."

The Other Children looked in wonder, waiting.

"How do you do, everyone," said the Balloon, trying to sound cheerful to please his Little Girl. "My name is Balloon. I belong to this Little Girl. We are very good friends."

"I'm pleased to make your acquaintance', he continued after a few seconds. "Could you all please tell me your names?"

None of the Other Children answered. They continued to watch him impatiently, leaving the Little Girl surprised.

"Balloon asked you to introduce yourselves," she added helpfully. "I know you've never heard a balloon talking, but it's only polite to answer his question."

The Other Children looked from the Little Girl to the Balloon and back. Then, they burst into laughter, and kept laughing and laughing.

"Let's get out of here," an Older Kid finally said. "We're wasting our time. I knew talking balloons were not real. It was just a hoax."

The Other Children scattered in every direction, elbowing each other and continuing to laugh.

The Little Girl was left alone in the deserted schoolyard, holding her Balloon by the string. What was going on?

Nobody had heard her Balloon speak. For everyone else, her Balloon was ordinary. Nice and big and green. Nothing but a colorful wrapping filled with air.

An Equation With Multiple Unknown Variables

"So, nobody except me sees my Balloon as anything but an ordinary green balloon. A beautiful balloon, it's true, but nothing more."

The Little Girl was in math class. The Teacher was talking about equations with two unknown variables, but she wasn't paying attention. Her little curly-haired head was lost in thought. She was trying to solve an equation with a far superior number of unknown variables.

"Was I wrong? Is my Balloon really anything more than a normal balloon, blown away in a park from a child's hand and stuck in a tree? Is he really my friend, or a beautiful and fragile toy, a simple colorful companion? I'm the only one who can hear him, and I'm the only one who can fly with him. Maybe everything was a dream. Who else has ever had something like this happen to them? Magical balloons like this one are only seen in books or on television."

The Little Girl clutched her head in her hands. "Oh, what a pity. It was such a nice game."

She tore a piece of paper from her notebook and started writing. Her soul was in tears. Lost in her own world, she wrote, and kept writing, even as the Teacher filled the blackboard with complicated equations with two unknown variables each.

The Letter

"My dear Balloon," the Little Girl said just before bed, looking into Balloon's big eyes. "Today I wrote you a letter. I left it open on my desk so you can read it while I sleep. You have all night. I know balloons don't sleep, they only take naps." She let out a long sigh.

"I'm sorry, my Balloon,
You have flown me to the Moon,
You've shown true friendship to me,
But real you cannot be."

On the Little Girl's desk, the letter stood open: a white paper covered in hurried writing.

39

Our Game

"My dear Balloon,

   I write this letter now for you, and for myself, so I can read it one day, long after the Balloon will have burst and the Little Girl will have stopped being a little girl (sadly, we both know this will happen sooner or later, as the rules of our different worlds dictate).

   I've wondered lately if you're real or simply a dream. A dream that I dreamt with my eyes wide open. My Dream. Now, unfortunately, I'm convinced that you're not real but only a figment of my imagination, starved as it is for beauty and adventure. I know I'm right, my dear Balloon. It's not because I want to be right, but because these are the laws of this world. You will agree with me, when it's time for you to return to Balloon Country. You will then understand that the time we spent together was but a game. That is why, sometimes – oftentimes – I doubted you and made you sad without meaning to. Because I, being sometimes a child, sometimes a little girl, know that games don't last forever. Then, my soul gets sad and starts to cry. As you keep reading, I wish for you to read the next lines affectionately and, maybe, with a tear hiding in the depths of your soul and the corner of your eye.

My most beloved green Balloon,

   I know this is just a game, but I want you to know that it was the best one I have ever played! We've been very happy together! I laughed and ran, holding you by the string, like I never did in any other game! We flew to the Rainbow Falls and I touched the clouds with my hands! You gave me a planet and made me a swing from your string and the Crescent Moon. Thank you for being mine for a little while and making my soul sing.

Your other half in Our Game,

Your Little Girl"

The Next Day

The next morning, Balloon was not there to wish her "Good morning, my Little Girl!' like he joyfully did every morning. He was not next to her bed. He was gone, nowhere to be seen. In his absence, the room was filled with an unnatural silence.

Where Are You?

"Where are you, Balloon? Do you hear me?' the Little Girl called, scared. "My Balloon, where could you have disappeared? Come back, my dear friend! I'm sorry, oh, I'm so sorry!"

She opened her window widely and looked around. The dawn of a beautiful summer day was settling on her street. The birds chirped, flowers bloomed and tiny bugs were putting on a concert in the tall grass.

The Balloon was nowhere in sight.

"Oh, what have I done? Oh no, what have I done?" she deplored through tears. "Balloon! Balloon! Ballooooon! Come back! Please, my Balloon, come back!"

The Flower-Filled Park

The Little Girl ran outside and looked all around. Not a trace of the Balloon could be seen. She sprinted towards the flower-filled park where she had first met the Balloon. The park was shining in the morning light, but today she didn't even notice its splendor. Her anxious eyes were searching everywhere for her dear Balloon: in the trees, through the tall grass, in the flowerbeds. She even looked through the thorny bushes, her heart tight in her chest with fear, scared to find him broken in one of them, without a trace of color – for, the Balloon, without the light of his eyes was a simple transparent covering.

But her Balloon was nowhere to be found.

The Little Girl collapsed on the ground, crying among the yellow, purple, red and pink flowers that blanketed the earth. Even the flowers, as chatty as we know them, were all suddenly silenced as though they were given a signal. A delicate butterfly, which moments ago had been proudly displaying his colors in flight, landed on a pansy to look at her. A big-bellied bumblebee hid inside another flower, and a curious ladybug landed on the Little Girl's raspberry-colored dress. A deep silence settled over the park. Even the cheerful breeze wrapped itself around the branch of a blooming lime tree, holding its breath.

"Chirp," said a little ash grey bird, landing next to the Little Girl.

"Chirp, chirp," was the answer, as others came down from all around.

They surrounded the Little Girl, watching her through eyes like shiny black pearls.

The Little Girl woke up amidst the flowers, birds, butterflies and little grass-dwelling bugs. They were all waiting for her to speak, to tell them her story.

And so, the Little Girl began recounting the most touching story in the world.

Our Story

There once lived a Little Girl.

One beautiful spring day, the Little Girl was happily walking through a park in full bloom. There, she saw a beautiful, big, green Balloon, perched in a tree. The Balloon was very excited to meet her. He immediately offered the Little Girl his string, knowing that she was the one for him. He told her: "I'm trusting you with my string. Never let it out of your sight. Whenever you need me, pull on it and I will be there."

The Little Girl couldn't help becoming fond of him from the moment she had seen him sitting in the tree with winking leaves. She let out a delighted "aah" knowing that from that moment on, her soul would never again be lonely.

The Balloon was a very cheerful fellow. He liked looking his best for his Little Girl, wearing a bowtie and a top hat.

They laughed a lot together. The Balloon was weak in the beginning. Any breath of air could blow him away. As their friendship grew, however, so did his strength. They started flying to the Rainbow Falls and back.

"We were very happy together," the Little Girl sighed after a while. "He was my Balloon and I was his Little Girl."

"If only you knew! He was a magic Balloon, one that cannot even be found in books or movies!" she told the birds, who were listening attentively.

"We did so many things together!"

"He threw his string
Away, to bring
A tiny star twinkling like gold,
For he and I to gently hold."

"He said that if I wished to swing,
He'd tie for me his balloon string
To a corner of the Moon.
And so I swayed just like a loon."

"A planet he offered to me,
So big it was! As it should be!
It's named after a god, you see,
So Jupiter had come to be,
Our little spot on the starry sea."

"This story is,
Odd it might sound,
Of me and a Balloon I found."

"But now I've lost him," she sobbed, hiccupping. "My Balloon went back to Balloon Country, or worse, has been popped. And it's entirely my fault! I didn't think he was good enough, I didn't love him like he deserved to be loved, I didn't protect him from the cruel world! My poor friend, where are you? What happened to you?"

"Oh my dear! Oh my dear!
Has my beloved, sunny Balloon,
Gotten popped just like I fear?"

"Wonder if he's gotten lost
Through the sky he loves the most?"

"Oh no, what have I done! Tell me, my friends, where should I look for my Balloon? How do I get to Balloon Country? I want to find him and bring him back!"

The Birds

Complete silence fell over the park. Even the big-bellied bumblebee, hidden as he was in his flower, drew back and kept silent.

"Chirp," said the little ash grey bird.

"Chirp, chirp," the other birds replied, their eyes shining like black pearls.

As though given a sign, they all took off, flapping their little wings, and formed a circle around the Little Girl. She felt them flutter close, and was not at all startled when they took her dress into their beaks and pulled her into the air. She felt herself rise and looked down to see her feet hanging and saw herself flying with the birds in the sky.

"Where are we heading?" she asked.

"Chirp, chirp," was the answer, and the Little Girl nodded her curly-haired head, pleased.

"We are going to Balloon Country? Thank you, my little friends! With your help, I will be able to find my beloved Balloon and bring him back!"

Balloon Country

In Balloon Country, everything was blue. The ground was blue. The sun was blue. The clouds were blue. The sky was, of course, blue. The balloons, however, were brightly colored with all the colors in existence. There were balloons which were red, pink, yellow, green, blue, orange, purple, brown, lilac and many more colors and shades. These Balloons were expressionless, with no shining eyes, they were nothing special. They scurried about in hurried groups as if they were very busy. They moved hectically, shaking their strings anxiously, and looked around frantically as if waiting for something, or someone.

Finding herself in the middle of this whirlwind of color, the Little Girl excitedly looked for her friend. There were many green balloons but not a single one looked even remotely like hers. Suddenly, she saw an emerald green balloon that was quickly moving away. She called: "Balloon, Balloon!" But the balloon didn't seem to hear her. She ran after it and grasped its string, tugging it to make it look at her. The balloon turned around and looked at the Little Girl holding onto his string. It was an ordinary balloon, like all the others around her. It wasn't her Balloon.

"Excuse me," the Little Girl said politely. "I thought you were someone else."

She tried to hide a tear that had appeared in the corner of her eye.

The balloon looked at her kindly, understandingly.

"Who did you mistake me for?" he asked curiously.

"I thought you were my friend, Balloon."

"Ah," he was disappointed. "I understand. You have your own balloon already," he sighed. "If you didn't have one I'd have offered to become yours. You see, here, we all wait for little boys and girls to take us to their world. It's sad in here, on our own."

"I'm sorry, Mister Balloon, I already have a balloon. He's special and wonderful and I don't want any other one. I hope you're not upset," she apologized, touched by the balloon's sadness.

"Of course, of course, it's no matter," he placated her. He hesitated a little then said: "You won't find your Balloon here. Once we find our child, we never come back to Balloon Country.

"Never?" she asked, scared.

61

"Never," he said firmly.

"What happens to you afterwards? I mean, after you leave here with your chosen little girl or boy?"

"That, I don't know," he said, with a shrug of his string – since balloons don't have shoulders. "None of us know. It's a mystery."

"It's a mystery for me as well," she whispered sadly. Being curious by nature, as you may remember, she continued: "Can you please tell me how balloons find their chosen owner?"

"That's another mystery," he sighed. "All we know is that, from time to time, some of us disappear from Balloon Country and go to Earth to meet our child. We never return."

The Little Girl was silent, concentrating. Many thoughts had formed in her curly-haired head. She suddenly brightened up. "I finally understand! Oh, it was right in front of me, how could I not see it? The balloons are not the ones that find the right child. It's the other way around. A boy or a girl on Earth wishes dearly for a certain balloon, and suddenly, it's snatched from Balloon Country and wakes up perched in a tree, surrounded by spring flowers. From there, the boy or girl collects it."

The emerald balloon was watching her perplexed, stone-still on his string.

"Balloon Country must be a dream garden, from which children collect colorful balloons. They pick them like flowers," she dreamily continued, a smile lighting up her face.

"Thank you, Mister Balloon! You were a great help. I hope you meet your little boy or girl soon!"

"Thank you, too, Little Girl," he answered ceremoniously. "Good luck! Don't give up! You will find your Balloon, I'm sure of it!"

The Dream

That evening, the little girl was finding it difficult to sleep. Late at night, when she finally fell asleep, she dreamed of her Balloon. It looked like he was being blown about by a strong wind and was quickly slipping away. Balloon was calling to her.

"Help! Help me, my Little Girl!" he was shouting in a scared and helpless voice. She was running, reaching for her Balloon as he was being blown further and further away. Once she caught up to him, she jumped to catch his string. However, it was now much shorter, almost nonexistent. The wind had stopped and the Balloon was dangling above her head but she couldn't catch him no matter how high she jumped. Suddenly, she heard laughing and was surrounded by her Classmates. They were making faces at her, pointing at her Balloon and laughing.

"Balloons go *POP*! Balloons go *POP*! Balloons go *POP*!"

"*POP*! *POP*! *POP*!"

The Little Girl woke up, scared and confused.

Back Together

"Good morning, my Little Girl!" a familiar little voice greeted her. The Little Girl jumped with surprise and joy at seeing her Balloon happily swaying at the foot of her bed. She quickly jumped out of bed and went to hug her friend. She held his big head between her hands and nuzzled his Balloon cheek. "My Balloon, I was so worried. I cried and looked everywhere for you. I searched all the places we had been to before, I even flew with the birds to Balloon Country to look for you, but I could not find you anywhere. Where did you disappear to, my dear Balloon? I was scared I had lost you forever."

The Balloon watched her for a few seconds, surprised, trying to understand what she was saying. He shook his big head slightly and answered:

"I never left, my Little Girl. I was always beside you. You could not see me because you stopped believing in me. I became invisible to you, as I am to all others who don't understand me."

He smiled warmly. "You should've simply looked for me closer to you: in your heart. You would've found me there immediately."

"My Balloon! My Balloon," cried the Little Girl. "Please forgive me for doubting you! I promise that, from now on, I will never let go of your string again! Only you can take me to the Rainbow Falls and back! Oh, Balloon, how I wish to fly with you again!"

"That's easy," he said, and bowed solemnly, swaying from right to left and from left to right on the end of his string, as we all know by now he does, when he's happy. "Allow me to get my top hat and fix my bowtie. Shall I offer you my string?"

The Little Girl smoothed her dress, adjusted her socks and polished her shoes.

"I am ready, Balloon!" she chirped happily.

"I am ready as well!" the Balloon called cheerfully. "Just say the magic words and we will take off together!"

"Come, Balloon,
Give me your string,
Let us fly and laugh and sing!

Go, Balloon,
Your string I hold,
Let us fly where dreams unfold!

Go, go, to the sky,
Let the wind make you fly,
Go above the earth and trees,
In the sky we feel at ease!

Now that we are back together,
You will be my friend forever!"

Made in the USA
Middletown, DE
05 March 2020

85893571R00042